NOTTING HILL CARNIVAL:
A WEST SIDE STORY

CANDICE CARTY-WILLIAMS

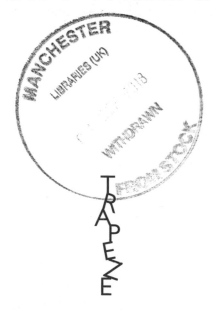

TRAPEZE

First published in Great Britain in 2020 by Trapeze
an imprint of The Orion Publishing Group Ltd
Carmelite House, 50 Victoria Embankment
London EC4Y 0DZ

An Hachette UK Company

1 3 5 7 9 10 8 6 4 2

A CIP catalogue record for this book is
available from the British Library.

ISBN (Paperback) 978 1 4091 9618 1
ISBN (eBook) 978 1 4091 9619 8

Typeset by Born Group
Printed and bound in Great Britain by Clays Ltd, Elcograf S.p.A.

www.orionbooks.co.uk

Chapter One

It was a Saturday, around 7 p.m. It was the twenty-seventh of August, and the eve of Notting Hill Carnival. The day had been sunny, and it wasn't getting dark any time soon. London was bristling with summer. The people, the trees, the sounds, they were all alive in a way that only summer can create. Summer gives life to things the other seasons can't fully nourish.

To begin our story, it makes sense to tell you who we're going to be following. A few years ago, two crews were formed. A crew of girls, led by Sapphire Light, who called themselves the Red Roses, and a crew of boys, led by Den Gold, who dubbed themselves the Gold Teeth.

The Red Roses were so named because they were, simply, Sapphire's flower of choice. The Gold Teeth were given their name because, simply, Den – Gold by name and nature – went to the dentist and was given three gold teeth at the age of fourteen. He thought it was pretty notable that every time he smiled he'd dazzle anyone looking his way.

1

Sapphire and Den were both fourteen years old, and in Year Nine at Brixton Park Manor. It was kind of a rough school where the teachers were too scared of the pupils to discipline them. Because they'd been there for a couple of years, they were both settled enough to think they had the run of the place.

At the beginning, they liked each other just fine. They wouldn't call themselves friends. But they definitely said, 'Y'alright, yeah?' to each other between classes, and if they happened to be in the same part of the playground at lunchtime.

One September day, though, the new Year Sevens, with their giant uniforms and even bigger rucksacks, came trotting into the school gates. Den and his friends (who weren't yet a crew) pointed at Kyla, a scruffy new starter whose whole uniform looked like one giant hand-me-down. The uniform was indeed a hand-me-down, from the blazer to the tights. They laughed at her hard enough that she felt her face turn hot. Instead of crying, she went to find her older sister, Sapphire. Kyla told Sapphire about the group of boys who had ruined her first morning, and went on with her day.

Sapphire, who was very, very protective, gathered the rest of her girls: Pinky, a tall, curvy girl with a huge smile; Katrina, as short as she was smart (very); Dee, whose name might have indeed been Dee or something longer (she never told anyone); and Charlotte, a hot-headed redhead.

They made their way over to Den, who was surrounded by his boys: Leon, stocky and with a pretty face, Zora Balvin (an honorary girl member because her twin brother, Apollo, who went to another school, was friends with Den) and Ricky, gangly and blonde, with a bad immune system. Francis was also present. He was Zora's boyfriend, completely devoted to her but had to pretend he wasn't in front of the boys. What Sapphire expected was a quick explanation from her and a quick apology from Den. But, this is how the conversation went:

Sapphire: You see that Year Seven you were rude to?
Den: Nah.
Sapphire: What d'you mean, 'nah'?
Den: I said what I said.
Sapphire: You know who I'm talking about.
Den: I've already told you I don't, man.
Zora: He already told you he doesn't.
Charlotte: You his puppet?
Zora: Who are you talking to?

Charlotte: You, I'm chatting to you.

Sapphire: Look, all I'm saying is that Year Seven is my little sister. Don't trouble her.

Den: I'll trouble who I want.

Sapphire: Why are you trying to look big and bad? Who you trying to impress?

Zora: He doesn't need to impress anyone.

Sapphire: Seems like he does. Anyway, we're gone. Remember what I said. You don't want no smoke, Den.

The girls walked away, ready to go to class. But then, Den shouted something at their backs that started something he could quite literally never finish:

Den: You think *I'm* going to listen to some ugly bitches?

Sapphire and the rest of the girls turned on their heels and walked back towards him.

Sapphire: I don't mind being called ugly, you know. What's ugly to you is beautiful to someone else. And I know we're all beautiful. But why you calling us bitches for? Why you on some beef tip? Nobody came here to fight you. You've got it now, though.

And from that point on, Brixton Park Manor became a sort of teenage verbal war zone for both crews, and any other pupil who got caught in the middle.

Fights, big and small, happened over the years, with only one ending in some real tragedy, but more about that a little later. The hate between both groups grew and grew, and turned into something much nastier than its origins. It's fair to say that nobody could really remember what happened at the beginning. But when you throw hormones and the stress of school and peer pressure into the mix, fiction becomes fact. Rumours and gossip become truths.

So, back to our story. As time went on, they got older. That's how time works, after all. Now that the Red Roses and the Gold Teeth didn't have school, and the few brave teachers who would step in to calm things down, their fight for power spilled out onto the streets of Brixton pretty much every other day. If it wasn't an argument on the corner by McDonald's, it was a scrap on the green by Windrush Square. They didn't care about passers-by, either. It was pretty much every person for themselves.

It's important to say that the Red Roses and the Gold Teeth weren't just about anger and small war. They were also friendship groups. They were about family. They were ride or die. More girls joined the Red Roses when others left, and more boys joined the Gold Teeth when others moved out of London. Each crew gained members, simply because there's always power in numbers.

So. The Red Roses and the Gold Teeth had roughly ten members each. Sapphire, now twenty, left the Red Roses two years ago. The Sapphire we come to now is a fairly quiet girl. She lives in a studio flat off Brixton Hill, and keeps herself to herself, apart from when she goes back to the family home to see her mum and sister. She got a job at a café in Brixton Market run by a woman called Dawn who is something of a community leader. Dawn is a stern Jamaican woman who does not suffer fools gladly, but runs her café with love.

Let me tell you about that fight at school, the one that ended in real tragedy. Sapphire had got into it with Ricky, one of the original Gold Teeth. Sapphire's sister Kyla was fifteen at this point. She was still wearing her sister's hand-me-down uniform, and had started spending a lot of time with a girl in her class called Katrina. They'd hold hands in the playground and when they left school.

Ricky took offence to that, for some reason.

One lunchtime, he shouted, 'Are you two gay or something?' across the playground when Kyla and Katrina had walked past. So Kyla had obviously gone to tell her sister rather than go and get lunch, which was the original plan.

By the time she found Sapphire, who was smoking behind the science block, the bell rang and it was time for class. Sapphire burst into three classrooms until she found Ricky in French. He was sitting at his desk and taking his textbook out of his bag. This is how the conversation went:

Sapphire: What's this you said to my sister?
Ricky: What?
Sapphire: You heard me.
Ricky: I didn't say nothing, man.
Sapphire: No, you did. You asked if she was gay.
Ricky: Well, so what if I did?
Sapphire: Well, so what if she is?

Ricky stayed quiet. None of his fellow Gold Teeth took French, so he had no backing.

Sapphire: I said, SO WHAT IF SHE IS, RICKY?

7

Ricky looked at the ceiling as the teacher backed out of the room to get help. She was a substitute teacher, so she *definitely* didn't know how to handle this.

Sapphire: What you've done is try to draw attention to something. You wanted to make people think that whatever my sister is doing is wrong. She's not doing anything wrong, Ricky. She's happy, Ricky. Are you? I don't think so, if you're shouting at people across the playground at your big age.
Ricky: It is wrong. It's weird.
Sapphire: Excuse you?
Ricky: I said it's weird.

Very wrong move from Ricky here. Sapphire dragged him out of his seat so that he was standing. Sapphire could feel the red mist rising. She'd been sent to the school counsellor for her behaviour enough times to know she should do her breathing exercises. But she was already past that point.

Sapphire: Call my sister weird *one* more time.

Ricky went to sit back down but he heard someone across the room laugh, and knew he needed to protect the reputation of his crew. He opened his mouth to repeat what he'd said. But, before he even got the word 'weird' out, Sapphire had delivered a blow to his jaw. This would usually have caused a bruise and a weird clicking noise when he opened his mouth. But, when Sapphire had hit him, Ricky had fallen backwards and cracked his head on the desk behind him.

Sapphire had been pulled out of the classroom, still trying to hit him. The ambulance had come. As well as the bruise and the weird clicking noise when he opened his mouth, Ricky was also now blind in one eye.

If she'd been a year younger, Sapphire would have ended up in a young offenders' unit for a year. But, because she'd turned eighteen by the time sentencing came around, she ended up in a women's prison. It was the most terrifying time of her life and she would never speak about it to anyone at all. It changed her, is all everyone knew. The red mist never came again.

Sapphire had handed the reigns of the Red Roses over to Pinky. When she'd been released, she wanted nothing more to do with it. She only endured any chat about it because her sister Kyla refused to leave. That was fine by Pinky, who was still about that rough and ready life. And she was secretly jealous that Sapphire, following her stint in prison, had more props than her.

Sapphire knew she could never go back to prison. She was determined to stay on the straight and narrow.

The head of the Gold Teeth was still Den, who was, as he always had been, on some sort of power trip. Den was a nasty piece of work, and had only got nastier as he'd grown up. It really wasn't his fault, though. As is so often the way, he'd grown up in a toxic household and didn't know who to talk to, or how to express his emotions. The older he got, the angrier he got at life, and blamed everyone around him for it. By the time he was twenty, he still lived at home. He barely spoke to anyone in the house, and spent most of his time roaming the streets with the Gold Teeth. He didn't have a job, though secretly he would have loved to work with animals. But nobody told him he could, so he didn't bother trying. Instead, he put all of his energy into starting fights, trying to recruit more Gold Teeth and cleaning his trainers.

Chapter Two

Anyway, so back to the story. One hot, late Saturday in August, on the eve of Notting Hill Carnival, Pinky and Kyla (who had very much grown into her own person, no more hand-me-downs) were on their way back to Pinky's. They had just collected the last of their Carnival uniform for the girls. In their bags were red rose print crop tops and fake red roses with clips attached for their hair. Kyla, always hungry or thirsty depending on the time of day, decided she wanted a drink. So she and Pinky took a detour, and ended up walking through an estate they usually only walked through when there were more of them.

'Look who it is,' they heard. They didn't turn around, because they knew the voice belonged to Zora, Apollo's twin sister. Zora, the only female member of the Gold Teeth, had become so used to being the only girl in a group of boys that she had incredible confidence. One people wanted to bottle and sell.

Pinky and Kyla carried on walking.

'What, you can't hear me?' Zora shouted after them, pushing the arm of her boyfriend Francis off her shoulders as she stepped forwards. She wasn't used to being ignored.

Pinky stopped walking and exhaled deeply. She had an overwhelming urge to turn to Kyla and say, 'Look. This is all because you're thirsty.' Instead, she turned around and followed where the voice had come from. Standing by a wall next to the recycling bins were Zora, Den and Leon. Three of the original Gold Teeth.

'I can hear you, Zora,' Pinky said. 'Can we help you?'

'Oi, this girl is asking if she can help me?' Zora laughed, looking at Den and Leon. 'You can help us by explaining why you're here.'

Pinky and Kyla watched as Zora's expression twisted itself from laughter into something more sinister.

'We don't need to explain anything to you,' Pinky said, turning back round, her bag of crop tops and roses swinging with her.

She and Kyla carried on walking ahead, picking up the pace. Zora didn't like that. She pushed herself off the wall and approached the girls from behind. She grabbed the bag from Pinky's hand, throwing it on the floor in one move.

12

'What you doing?' Kyla shouted, pushing Zora. Kyla was very fiery. Less so than her sister used to be, but still, very fiery. The second her hands made contact with Zora's shoulders, Kyla knew she'd made a wrong move.

Within seconds, almost all of the rest of the Gold Teeth emerged from various shadows on the estate, and moved towards the girls.

Pinky and Kyla knew what to do. They ran, but not before picking up the bag. That was a priority. Side by side, they pounded the pavements in Nike trainers that were only for show and not for any actual running. They never looked at each other, only looked back to see that they were still being chased.

'I can't keep going!' Kyla panted.

'I bet you could use that drink now!' Pinky panted back. 'Look, we're almost at the bus stop, we can jump on that 159!'

But before they could get to the bus stop, they bumped, quite literally, into two police officers. And those two loved nothing more than to patrol the area and either belittle or patronise the young people who lived there.

'And what might you two be running from?' The question came from one of the officers. He was a plump man with pasty skin and a moustache that seemed to be modelled on someone from the eighties.

He didn't need an answer when he saw one girl and eight boys run around the corner.

'It's the same thing as usual, I see,' sighed the second officer, a tall and thin man who was as pasty as his sidekick but with no facial hair. He reached for his baton. 'You lot are the ruin of this area.'

Zora, who was well known by the officers, stopped when she saw them. The last time she was involved with them she ended up in a cell for a night. There was no way she was missing Carnival the next day.

'Hold back, hold back,' she said to the boys.

'Two options,' Moustache Officer shouted so that everyone he was addressing could hear. 'I watch you all shake hands and go your separate ways, or I take you all in. Your choice.'

'What you taking us in for?' Den shouted back.

'Disturbing the peace,' Non-Moustache Officer called out.

'That's not even a thing, is it?' Den laughed.

'It's what I say it is,' Non-Moustache Officer laughed back.

The next few minutes were a joke. Pinky and Kyla had to stand next to the officers while the nine members of the Gold Teeth lined up the way a football team do at the beginning of a match, and shook their hands. When Zora, last in the line, got to Pinky, she looked her dead in the eye and told her, 'This isn't over.'

'Correct,' Pinky smiled. 'It'll be over when we end it.'

'What was that?' Moustache Officer asked.

'Nothing, officer,' Pinky said. 'I just told Zora here that we'll be seeing her at Carnival tomorrow. That's all.'

That unofficial invitation did four things:

- Made Pinky realise that pride very much comes before a fall.
- But also let her show everyone how hard she was. Swings and roundabouts.
- Gave Zora such intense blood pressure that she vowed that she and the Gold Teeth were going to Carnival. And she would make sure she messed Pinky up so badly that the Red Roses would have no choice but to get rid of her as leader.
- Made sure that both officers got back in their cars when everyone cleared off. And then sorted it with their chief that they'd cover Notting Hill Carnival that weekend. And there they would finally lock up

every member of the Red Roses and the Gold Teeth the second they kicked off.

When they finally got back to Pinky's, and Kyla had her drink, of course, Pinky called an emergency Red Roses meeting. When everyone was there, gathered in the tiny kitchen, and Pinky's mum had taken herself to bed, Pinky sat on the kitchen counter and addressed her girls.

'As some of you know, because *one* of us doesn't know anything about *waiting* for what they want, Kyla and I almost got *got* today. We need to sort this shit out with them Gold Teeth. These ends are too small for two of us to go out alone. Take one wrong turn and God knows what happens.'

'Er, can I just cut in?' Kyla said quietly, draining her carton of Ribena loudly. 'As much as I might have got us there, *you're* the one who told them *all* that we were going to be at Carnival tomorrow.'

'Classic Pinky,' Katrina, Kyla's girlfriend, said. 'Selective memory.'

Pinky jumped down from the kitchen counter and walked over to Katrina slowly. 'I don't care if you're Kyla's girlfriend. You and me are not size. Remember your place.'

Katrina went to roll her eyes but looked at the floor instead. Kyla placed a supportive hand on Katrina's knee.

Pinky went back to the kitchen counter and jumped up. 'Any suggestions? I don't think we can take them on ourselves. But I still think we should handle it ourselves. We need to get smart.'

'We should talk to Sapphire,' Kyla said.

Now. Pinky didn't like this. She had fought for her position as leader since Sapphire left. She didn't need any suggestion that she hadn't been good enough. But, instead of saying how displeased she was, she kept quiet. Kyla, being Sapphire's sister, got special treatment.

Instead, Pinky smiled and asked, 'What's Sapphire gonna do?'

'Well, she was there in the beginning,' Kyla said.

'I was there in the beginning,' Pinky reminded her, and everyone else. 'Right next to her, when this all began. Because they were starting on you, lemme add right quick.'

'Yeah but you know what I mean,' Kyla began. 'Sapphire isn't like us any more. She's smart, she knows how to sort things out.'

Chapter Three

'Who hasn't got their grills?' Den asked his boys and Zora from the beaten armchair in the corner of his tiny living room. Den, suitably, was the only member of the Gold Teeth who actually had real gold teeth. Zora planned to get hers fitted soon.

All of the other members, squashed into the small room, flashed their fake gold smiles. Den was almost blinded by the result as the light from the lamp bounced off the grills and dazzled him.

'Right, so we're ready for tomorrow yeah?' he asked as he stood up, and was answered with various 'yeahs' and nods.

'We aren't . . . fighting females though?' Leon asked. He was raised with four sisters. Even though he knew they could handle themselves, he was sick to his stomach at the idea of any man ever laying a hand on a woman.

'Nah, it's going to be me and that Pinky prick,' Zora said, standing up. 'I know a couple of girls round the way I can bring with me to fight in case the others jump in. But it should be me and her.'

'You're not the leader to make that call, you know,' Den said. 'I say I fight her, finish her, it is *over*.'

'This isn't your fight, Den,' Zora protested. Sadly for Zora, having seen a *lot* of shit growing up, she wasn't phased by a man and a woman fighting. But this fight was about *her*. It was about power. She'd been walking in Den's shadow for way too long. She needed the others to see that, even though she was a girl, she had to be taken seriously.

'All right, let's put it to a vote then,' Den shrugged, confident that he'd have full support from his boys. 'All who want me to put that Red Rose in her place, raise a hand.'

He looked around and saw that only three of the Gold Teeth were backing him. 'What the fuck? You man getting moist in your old age?'

The others looked at the floor.

'Leon? Not even *you*?' Den asked his longest-standing friend.

'Listen, man, you know I got you, but you know I got sisters, innit?' Leon shook his head. 'It's not the same and you know it. We're not in school any more. Me and you bang gym like, every day. If you hit that girl the wrong way, you could kill her.'

'Francis, man? Come on,' Den said.

Francis laughed in response. He was still completely devoted to Zora and everyone knew it.

'Where's Apollo?' Den asked, kissing his teeth and throwing himself back into the armchair. 'Only need one more vote.'

'He's on the balcony, but, but, that's not how voting works?' Zora laughed. 'If me and Den don't vote, four votes and four votes is a tie.'

'Yeah but I'm the leader, so I make the final call,' Den smiled before getting up and walking out into the hallway. 'Apollo!'

'That's dumb and you know it.' Zora narrowed her eyes at him. 'Plus, my brother, my *twin*, ain't gonna back you over me.'

'Don't be so sure,' Den told her, taking his seat again.

'Yo.' Apollo strolled into the living room slowly, leaning against the wooden drinks cabinet.

'What you doing on the balcony?' Den asked. 'Nothing to see round here but the estate.'

'I like it.' Apollo shrugged. 'You called?'

'Who's fighting Pinky tomorrow?' Den asked. 'Me or Zora?'

'Zora, if anyone,' Apollo said immediately.

'Thank you,' Zora said, smugly. 'I told you he'd back me.'

'It's not even about backing you, bro,' Apollo said. 'Why'd you want to fight a woman?'

'Them Red Roses are always scrapping. They're not regular girls, man. They're like mandem,' Den said. 'Remember what that one did to Ricky?'

'Nope.' Apollo shook his head as he turned to walk out of the room. 'Anyway, I'm gonna kick. See you at home, Z.' He wasn't one for story time all the time.

Sapphire sat in the back room of Dawn's café. She was trying to make her way through the day's takings. She didn't really have a head for numbers, but she'd pushed on, and was able to handle the accounts without Dawn checking on her any more.

Sapphire heard a knock on the door of the café. She stopped counting the money and stayed completely silent.

The knock on the café door came again, louder this time. She quickly placed all the money in the old metal takings box, and got up. She went over to the wall opposite, lifted a framed picture of a beach in Jamaica from it and placed it on the floor slowly. Behind the picture was a safe that she opened as quietly as she could. She placed the box in, closed it even more quietly than she'd opened it, then hung the picture back on the wall. She crept back to her seat. They'd never been robbed before, but Sapphire's days in the Red Roses meant that she could immediately be on high alert.

A bang on the door again. Sapphire, who could always draw on the Sapphire she was before, reached under the desk and felt for the aluminium baseball bat that Dawn used as their unofficial safety system. Sapphire swung the bat around twice for practice, then headed out of the office into the dark café. The shutters were closed, so she waited for the knock to come again before shouting out, 'What the fuck do you want?'

She heard two bursts of laughter before unlocking the door and yanking it open.

'You two are lucky I didn't come out swinging this bat,' she said. 'Why you coming here so late? Trying to give me a heart attack.'

'Who can give the great Sapphire Light a heart attack?' Pinky said, moving past Sapphire and stepping into the shop. Kyla followed and immediately went to the fridge to get a drink.

Sapphire watched them both, blinking slowly. She sighed and closed the door behind them, locking it again.

'We have a problem,' Kyla said, sipping from a tin of Ting. 'Pinky has got us into a problem.'

'Why you telling me for?' Sapphire asked, crossing her arms. 'I'm not into this madness any more. I don't care who got who into what.'

'It's them stupid Gold Teeth. They started it,' Pinky told Sapphire. She explained what had happened that day, with Kyla acting out certain bits. She thought that Sapphire might feel involved enough to want to help them if she saw it played out.

'All I'm hearing is that you need to chat to Zora and squash it,' Sapphire said, once show and tell was over. 'What's the point in this? We're too old for this, man. Carnival is for enjoyment and family fun, and you lot are wanting to go all the way to west London for some big rumble? Could never be me. Chat to her, squash it, end it.'

'I'm not backing down like that!' Pinky said, horrified.

'OK. Well how about if you don't back down you're going to get fucked up. *Plus* I forbid my sister from going?' Sapphire asked.

'OK. You're right. I'll end it,' Pinky said, quickly enough to make Sapphire a bit unsure. It wasn't like Pinky to back down. 'Will you come, though?'

'Come where?' Sapphire asked.

'Carnival tomorrow,' Pinky said. 'I need that support, need that calm energy from you.'

'Me?' Sapphire yelled. 'Me? No way. This weekend is my only two days off in one hundred years, and getting it was *tough* because it's the bank holiday weekend. I've got shit to do.'

'Like what?' Kyla asked, excited by the idea of spending a day out with her big sister. She never saw her any more.

'Like, got to get my hair done? Wash my clothes? Chores? Errands?' Sapphire listed.

'You can get your hair done on Monday, and I'll wash your clothes and all that on Tuesday, sis!' Kyla promised.

Sapphire paused to think. She *did* spend all her time at work or in bed sleeping; it might be good to get out of South even if it was for a day. Plus, if anything was going to kick off, at least she could be there to protect her sister.

'Fine. But I'm not wearing the Red Roses uniform,' Sapphire said. 'Never again.'

'Deal,' Pinky said, smiling.

Chapter Four

The day had finally arrived. And it was raining. It was absolutely pouring. Nobody had expected this, and absolutely nobody knew how to dress for this. Half of the Red Roses were getting ready at Pinky's, and the other half were meeting them at Brixton tube station.

'Wait, so what, what do we do? Do we just wear our clothes and get wet?' Katrina asked, carefully pulling her rose-patterned top over her freshly styled hair.

'What?' Pinky asked. 'Have you never been out in the rain before?'

'No, obviously I've been out in the rain before, but I know how serious you take this uniform stuff.' Katrina sighed. Pinky was already getting het up and they weren't leaving the house for another hour. 'The last time we went to Carnival, you sent me home because I forgot my red bandana!'

'This is different,' Pinky said. 'You can just wear a coat and take it off when it stops raining. I feel like that's basic sense.'

'You don't need to be patronising anyone on this most sacred of days!' Kyla swept into the room spraying deodorant under her arms. 'I know you're stressing but leave my girlfriend alone. She only wants to check.'

Pinky rolled her eyes and started looking for her phone. 'Kyla, you heard from Sapphire?'

'She's meeting us there,' Kyla said, standing in front of the mirror and clipping roses in her hair.

'Meeting us *there*?' Pinky asked. 'When she lives round the corner? She's *choosing* to meet us in a crowd rather than just travelling with us?'

'Yeah, Dawn needs her to open up or something,' Kyla said. 'It's fine, you know Sapphire knows her way about the place.'

Pinky carried on getting ready in the bathroom so that she had a bit of space to breathe. As she did, she noticed that her hands were shaking. Was she nervous? She didn't want to think about it. 'Whatever would happen would happen' is the only thing that she allowed herself to think.

At midday, ten girls dressed in various styles of coat and under various styles of umbrella (though strictly red) met outside Brixton tube station. Once they got into the station, they removed all of their wet weather gear. Red rose printed crop tops, jeans, red trainers and fake red roses in their hair were revealed. They headed to Holland Park tube station.

At a quarter past twelve, just fifteen minutes later, nine boys and a girl, none with umbrellas but all wearing the same blue and gold Nike windbreaker, all with real or pretend gold teeth, met outside Brixton tube station. They headed to Holland Park tube station.

Apollo, despite being Zora's twin brother, was very much his own person and an 'opt-in, opt-out' member of the crew. This had always been the case since he went to a different school to everyone else. It helped that he wasn't always there to see the ins and outs of what went on between Sapphire and her girls and Den and his boys. But he also just thought it was a bit silly. He couldn't take it seriously and did it for his sister, mainly. He'd nod along, while reading a book, when she spoke about this girl 'who needed to get a punch in her face' and that girl 'who was going to catch a bang to the throat'.

Today, he'd finally decided to join them. Carnival was a special occasion, after all. Much like in the Red Roses, there was clearly some sort of crew rule that meant siblings got special treatment.

Apollo had a lot of presence. He wasn't especially tall or built, nor was he facially very striking, but there was something about him that made you stop and think about him for a second. Then stop and think about him again. Then think about him later. It might have been his eyes, which seemed to look through you. Or it was in the way that he moved, maybe. He carried himself gracefully, a bit like he was better than any of his surroundings.

He and Zora didn't look especially similar, either, and that may have been something to do with how they were as people. While Zora was driven by power, Apollo was driven by knowledge. Zora was a doer, Apollo was an observer.

'I know you don't have your Oyster,' Zora said across the barriers as she watched her brother searching all of his pockets. 'I don't even know why you're looking.'

'I know it's here, I swear I put it – aaah.' Apollo closed his eyes as he saw himself reach past the coat his Oyster card was always in and choose his windbreaker instead. 'OK, lemme go back and get it. I'll meet you lot there.'

'How you gonna find us?' Zora asked.

'Phones?' Apollo shrugged, turning to leave the station.

'You are so bad at your phone!' Zora called towards his back as he bounced up the steps to the street.

The way that public transport works, both crews reached Holland Park tube around five minutes apart, with the Gold Teeth arriving first. There'd been a lot less faff on their journey, plus they moved faster and with more purpose than the Red Roses.

Sapphire finally made it to Brixton station an hour after the rest of the girls had met. She'd decided that she was absolutely not going to wear red. Instead, she wore a tight black tracksuit. Neutral, comfortable, pretty good in the rain.

She checked her phone to see where she was going, pulled her headphones on and made her way down into the underground. She was first onto the carriage so she got a seat. She had five stops to go, so she spread out so that nobody would sit next to her. She was a black girl in a tracksuit, so already knew that nobody would sit next to her anyway.

She turned her music up and closed her eyes, thinking about how much damage control she was going to have to do later that day. She loved Pinky like a sister, but she also knew how completely *reckless* Pinky could be. Sapphire never led the Red Roses into trouble like this, because she knew just how much it took to keep the peace. And how one small thing could disrupt it.

Apollo, as he always did, ran down the escalator, weaving his body around the people making their way to the platform, got to the bottom and saw a fairly full carriage. He made a run for it and jumped on, squeezing through the doors as they closed on him. The hood of his windbreaker got caught, so he pulled himself through with such gusto that he ended up falling onto someone.

A girl, the most beautiful he'd ever seen, he realised very quickly, looked up at him and narrowed her big brown eyes. She pushed him off her and crossed her arms and legs.

'Sorry, sorry,' he mouthed, looking around. There were no free seats so he backed up and leant against the doors so he could take this girl in. Her black hair, parted in the middle, was gelled down and pulled into a mass of tight curls at the base of her neck.

Her eyebrows, thick and precise, framed her heart-shaped face. Her face was full, her lips plump. Apollo's pull to her was so instant that he wondered if they'd met before. He looked at the floor before looking up slowly to check that she wasn't looking at him. Her eyes were closed and she was nodding along to whatever she was listening to. The next stop was Stockwell. He hoped that the person opposite her got up

30

so that he could sit in that seat and take her in fully, maybe catch her eye.

He wasn't the kind of guy to just *talk* to girls on the street, or in this case, the tube. He'd never really had anyone he could have called a girlfriend in the twenty years he'd been on this planet. But he had kind of fallen into situationships here and there, before realising he just wasn't ever getting the kind of conversation or connection he craved.

Sex wasn't a big deal for him either. He'd had it, and enjoyed it, sure, but it wasn't the thing that drove him to talk to girls. He didn't really know what his driver was with girls at this point. For now, he was happy working in the record shop at the end of his road. 'Music!' he thought; that's how he could get talking to her. He knew a lot about music.

Stockwell came and went, and the person opposite the girl didn't get off. So did Vauxhall, Pimlico, Victoria and Green Park, and he knew he had to get off at Oxford Circus, the next stop. He clenched his fists, building up his courage.

He didn't want to make her take off her headphones. He knew it was too loud to talk to her properly, and he definitely did not want to get rejected in front of everyone on the tube. Why did he care so much, he wondered. Who even was this girl to spin his head like this? He thought about writing his number on a piece of paper or something. Surely that's what people did in this situation? Even though he knew he didn't have a pen or even a piece of paper to write on, he patted all of his pockets. And patted them ever more madly as he realised that, when he'd gone back home for his Oyster card, he'd left his phone on the stairs. Of all the days to leave his phone at home.

Sapphire opened her eyes and saw the boy by the doors, who had first fallen on her and had then done a bad job of spying on her, moving in a weird way. Was he . . . dancing? No. Was he itching himself? He wasn't.

She pulled up her hood as she stood up to get off at the next stop. She saw him stop moving and stare at her, his bright eyes flashing as he took her in. She raised her eyebrows at him and turned around as the tube came to a slow stop and the doors opened. She walked towards the Central line in time with her music and stopped as she felt a hand on her shoulder.

She tensed up and turned slowly, pulling her hood down and coming face to face with the boy from the tube.

'Can I help you?' she asked, not smiling, not frowning, not anything. Just a neutral face.

'Do I know you from somewhere?' he said back, smiling.

Sapphire stifled a laugh. This was the oldest trick in the book, though she hadn't heard it for a long time. All work and no play in the last few months had made Sapphire feel like nobody would ever be attracted to her.

'I don't think so,' she smiled. He was kind of cute. Not as big as the guys she usually went for, but she did like his eyes.

'You from here?' he asked her.

'You like a lot of questions! Do you mean am I from Oxford Circus?' Sapphire asked, moving out of the way of her fellow travellers.

'Ha, no, I mean Brixton,' he said. 'Where I fell on you. Sorry about that.'

'No harm, no foul,' Sapphire told him, checking her phone. At least a million messages from Kyla asking where she was. Surely trouble hadn't started already?

'Yeah. Brixton born and bred. Anyway. I should go, I'm running late.'

'Oh, right. OK, cool. Well, nice to have met you,' Apollo smiled. This girl wasn't into it and he wasn't going to push it. 'Have a good day, yeah.'

'And you.' Sapphire nodded, pulling her hood back up. She waved a goodbye, speed-walked and then burst into a full run towards the Central line.

Apollo stood for a few seconds and watched Sapphire as she sped off. If anything, talking to her had made him even more certain that she was really about it. He didn't know what to do with this feeling.

When Sapphire arrived at Holland Park and stepped out onto the pavement, the sun streamed onto her face. She stopped and looked around at all of the beautiful people making their way to where the fun was happening.

Everyone but her was dressed brightly, face paint or glitter smeared either expertly or sloppily onto their faces. It didn't matter how it was applied, they all looked so happy. As they all headed to the heart of things, people's spirits were as bright as the vibe itself.

Sapphire pulled her phone out again and saw that she had a video from Kyla. She held her breath as she opened it, expecting the worst. Bracing herself for blurry scenes of total fighting chaos, she exhaled as she instead saw a video of Kyla and the rest of the girls dancing and laughing.

Grateful that nobody was in danger, Sapphire calmed herself. She pulled her jumper off and wrapped it around her waist.

'Should have known you were coming here. Not really dressed for it, are you?'

Sapphire looked round to where the voice had come from. Tube boy.

'Are *you*?' she asked him.

'This is the uniform,' Apollo told her, pointing at his windbreaker. 'If I could have chosen, I would have dressed like that.' He pointed at a woman strutting past in a brightly coloured, feathered and jewelled full Carnival costume.

Sapphire laughed. 'What float you on? Mandem float?'

'Oh, you've got jokes?' Apollo smiled.

Sapphire actually wondered if she'd met *him* before.

'Do you know where you're going?' she asked him. 'I've got to meet my sister by some stage. I dunno where it is, though.'

'Now,' Apollo began, 'and you can definitely say no, cause we've just met each other. And I don't even know your name – I'm Apollo by the way. But I forgot my phone at home and don't even know where I need to go to meet my sister. If I plot about with you, I might find her.'

'Apollo. That's a nice name,' Sapphire said. 'Sure. Stick with me. You might have to fight at some point, let me warn you.'

'Fight *you*?' Apollo laughed. He was so relieved that she hadn't sent him away that he forgot to ask what her name was.

'Not me! Don't worry about it,' Sapphire said. She didn't want to scare him off. He seemed like a legit guy.

And so, they walked, in the sun, through the crowds of excited people, talking as they did. They passed the dancing people on floats, vibing out to reggae, ragga and soca, the beats mingling in the air to create one joyous Carnival sound. They passed the street vendors, all selling the most delicious-smelling food. When they stopped to look, they saw stalls of fresh fruit, stalls that had big round pans full of chicken, rice, curry goat. Their mouths watered when they saw the round, flaky rotis and the big vats of fruit punch.

As they moved through the vibrant and busy streets, Apollo asked Sapphire what she was listening to. When she told him she was listening to John Holt, he told her that *1000 Volts of Holt* was the only album he listened to regularly. He asked her where she worked. And when she told him, he said that even though Dawn's café was on the way to the record shop he worked in, he'd never been in.

They carried on talking about this and that, both asking questions to slyly find out:

- Whether or not the other was single (yes)
- Whether or not the other was straight (yes)
- Whether or not the other had children (no)
- How many siblings the other had (one sister each)
- Where their families were from (Jamaica, Grenada)
- Where exactly the other lived (Elm Park, Jebb Avenue, i.e. close)
- What the other liked to do in their spare time (sleeping, gym)
- Where they went to school (Brixton Park Manor, County Grange)
- If their parents were still together (no, not at all)

A while into walking and talking, Apollo asked Sapphire if she was hungry.

'Not hungry *hungry*, but I could eat,' she said.

Apollo took Sapphire's hand and guided her through the crowd. Before they found it, they smelled exactly what they both wanted. They followed their noses until they saw a laughing man open a jerk drum and flip the chicken inside.

Salivating, they got in the queue, standing closer and closer to each other as they discussed what they were going to get. Apollo wanted to put his arm around Sapphire, but knew that was *way* too familiar. Boundaries and that.

When they got their food, they sat on the side of the road and ate slowly. Both were aware that, even though they almost kind of felt like they'd known each other for ages, they were still strangers, and food all over their faces wasn't a good look at this point.

'What time is it?' Apollo asked. 'My sister is going to kill me.'

'How old is your sister?' Sapphire asked. 'Oh hold on, you've got—'

Sapphire used her thumb to wipe a glob of ketchup from just above Apollo's jawline.

'Sorry!' she yelped. 'That was too touchy of me! I should have just told you!'

'Ha, don't worry,' Apollo laughed, embarrassed. 'I liked it.'

'Oh shit,' Sapphire said, taking her phone out of her pocket. 'It's quarter past three.'

She checked the messages that she'd accidentally been ignoring, and saw that she had a code red from Kyla.

'I'm sorry, I've got to run,' Sapphire told Apollo, who couldn't hide his immediate and crushing disappointment.

'But, but—' he started. But she cut him off by kissing him square on the mouth. He felt his chest tighten. He didn't want her to go.

'Long to explain!' she shouted, and with that, she disappeared.

'I didn't even get your name,' Apollo said, as he watched the crowd swallow her up.

Chapter Five

The two crews had finally come face to face by the Aba Shanti-I stage. Den had been trying desperately to dance with about three girls (none of them were interested). Then he had seen Katrina and Kyla coming back from the toilets and had messaged Zora, who wasn't far away. Den had trailed after them, keeping a close eye on their red rose tops, keeping Zora updated.

Zora and the rest of the Gold Teeth caught up with Den the Spy a few minutes later.

'There they all are,' Den had smiled, licking his lips. 'All the Red Roses in one place, ready for us.'

'Ready for me, you mean,' Zora had said, stepping forwards.

The Red Roses had clocked the Gold Teeth and had made sure that everyone was present, alert and ready before getting ready to square up.

The two crews circled each other steadily, at first silent – intimidation tactic 101 that both sets had learnt from their schooldays – then they began to goad each other.

'This is what you asked for!' Den had shouted at Pinky. 'You lot can't be scared now.'

'Scared of who?' Pinky shouted back. 'Scared for what?'

Dancing strangers in the crowd, who were sober enough to realise what was going on, had backed off. Others had carried on dancing, not understanding that if these two crews got going, they didn't care about anyone who got caught in the middle.

Pinky had squared her shoulders, then stepped into the space in the middle of everyone. 'It's you I'm here for!' she'd shouted at Zora.

'Come then!' Zora had bellowed back, throwing herself at Pinky.

This is when Sapphire had arrived, sweating and panting.

'Come on, you two!' Sapphire shouted at the two girls in the middle of the circle. 'This day ain't about this!'

The two girls ignored her at first, circling each other. Zora threw up a boxer's stance, and Pinky copied her.

'Nah.' Sapphire said, pushing her way through and standing in the middle of them. 'You lot aren't serious. Next thing you know this is on the internet. No, it's in the *papers*, and you've got everyone saying that Carnival isn't safe and that all of us are hooligans.'

'Look who we've got here,' Officer Moustache seemed to say in delight, stepping into the middle of the circle. 'The Red Roses and the Gold Teeth. Doing exactly what they do best.'

Sapphire groaned. This officer was her absolute ruin. He'd known her as trouble back in the day, and would never let her move past it. At least every two weeks he'd 'pop' into Dawn's café to check that she was behaving herself, like an unofficial parole officer.

'Why are you even here?' she asked him. 'Bit far for you, isn't it?'

'We've got a nose for trouble, Sapphire,' Non-Moustache Officer told her. 'And you lot leave quite the smell.'

'OK, well I'm sorting it. It's fine. No trouble here,' Sapphire said.

'I think that's for us to decide, isn't it?' Moustache Officer told her. He looked around in a way that he'd decided was menacing but really wasn't. The others mainly ignored him.

Apollo, who had run to follow Sapphire, stood outside the circle and watched the whole thing.

'Where've you been, man?' Den asked, spotting him and pulling him into the circle. 'Look at this girl, coming like some community activist or whatever. You never would have known *big bad* Sapphire, leader of the Red Roses, would be the one to be so soft.'

'*Old* leader!' Pinky shouted back, even though she had two officers next to her. Pinky's pride never slept.

On hearing her name, Sapphire turned to look at Den. She looked at Apollo next to him. Then looked around the circle and realised that his jacket was identical to everyone else's. Her pounding heart sank in her chest.

'Please don't listen,' she mouthed at him, sadly.

Apollo looked back at her, not knowing what to say, or how he could even say it while everyone was around. All he did know was that the feeling he'd had when he'd seen her on that tube wouldn't budge. And he couldn't ignore it. He knew it had to mean something.

'Right, look, just break it up, all right?' Officer Moustache said. He knew there was no point trying to arrest any of them. The paperwork would be a nightmare this weekend. 'But I'll be watching. And I won't hesitate to make sure you, Sapphire, are chucked back in the cell you left two years ago.'

Everyone carried on basically ignoring him.

'Please. We've got a bad rep as it is, can't you

43

see that?' Sapphire pleaded with Zora.

'All right, do you know what?' Zora said, dropping her fists finally. 'Fine, you have a point. We'll go. You lot go and have your little fun today. We'll head out. But we discuss it tonight, back on ends.'

'Where?' Pinky asked.

'What kind of discussion are we talking?' Sapphire asked. 'Discussion with talking or discussion with hands?'

Zora looked at Pinky. 'Just talking,' she said. She was just as good a liar as Pinky was.

'Just talking,' Pinky nodded slowly, also lying.

'OK, we all meet in the courtyard outside Dawn's café at midnight,' Sapphire said. 'You lot know we can't keep on like this.'

'Aight. Let's scatter,' Zora said, walking out of the circle and into the crowd. The Gold Teeth, including her twin, Apollo, followed her.

Den shook his head as he walked away. He wasn't a follower, *he* was the leader. This girl was getting too above her stations, he thought. There was no *way* things were ending without his say.

Sapphire threw her head back and let out a scream of frustration before she faced Pinky.

'You told me to come here because you were going to end it, but you wanted me to come here

44

to back you? I'm not going back to pen! Not for you, not for the Red Roses, not even for my sister!' she shouted. 'Did you know about this, Kyla?'

'No!' Kyla protested. 'I didn't know anything! You know Pinky does what Pinky wants to do!'

'No, Pinky wants to run the Red Roses to make sure that everybody is scared of us!' Pinky shouted.

'People being scared? What's with your obsession with being top don?' Sapphire asked Pinky. 'I know you think you're tough because you can talk the talk and you can throw a few punches. But you haven't seen the things I've seen, Pinky! You need to settle down!'

'I need to settle down?' Pinky shouted. 'It's all fine for you, Sapphire! You're out of this life. You've got a job, you've got money. All I've got going for me is my name and the Red Roses! And I'm going to make sure everyone respects me, respects us! You think it's easy for a group of girls to keep themselves safe in ends? You know how many times Kyla and Katrina have been harassed, how many times Charlotte got harassed before she left London? You're the one who got out! You don't know what it's like!'

'I didn't get *out*, Pinky. I went to prison because I hit some boy so hard he can't see properly! Why don't you see how bad that is?

45

Why do you want to make the mistakes I did? Why do you want to be the old me?'

'I'm not trying to be like the old you, Sapphire,' Pinky said. 'I'm going to be *better* than you. Everyone is going to remember my name. And my name is going to make them tremble.'

Sapphire and Pinky stared at each other, anger rising and rising in their chests.

'I'm gone,' Sapphire said, breaking the silence. 'At midnight, you lot come to Dawn's. I'm ending this gang shit. Properly.'

'You don't have the right,' Pinky laughed.

'I started the Red Roses,' Sapphire corrected her. 'All of this? Came from me. I'll always have the power. And if you don't like it? I'll fight you for it.'

Sapphire turned and walked away. She knew it wouldn't take much more for the old her to appear.

'Oi, what was that girl saying to you?' Den asked Apollo once they'd all found somewhere else to dance. 'Swear she was saying something.'

'Which girl?' Apollo asked, trying to stall giving Den an answer.

'That Sapphire girl. The one who went pen few years ago. The only girl I've ever been shook of,' Den laughed.

'What?'

'Remember when Ricky got in that fight and ended up half blind?'

'Ricky who got sent to live with his grandparents in Wales or whatever?' Apollo remembered.

'Yeah, his parents overreacted innit,' Den laughed. 'Anyway, it was Sapphire who did it.'

'Rah,' Apollo said, shaking his head. 'How come I never saw her?'

'You know you're here, there and everywhere, man. By the time you started rolling with us a bit more she was locked up. Then she left Red Roses. You didn't answer the question, though.'

'What question?' Apollo asked, dodging the question yet again.

'What was she saying to you?' Den pushed.

'Nothing. I don't know her,' Apollo said.

'Whatever. Need to go toilet,' Den said, leaving Apollo with nothing but his thoughts.

Apollo felt this intense conflict inside him. He hadn't ever felt especially tied to the Gold Teeth, but his sister was his sister. He couldn't overlook that. But this girl Sapphire, she was really something. They'd only spoken for a few hours, but it was more than that. He felt like he properly knew her. He hadn't felt a connection like this in his life. Sure, he was only twenty, but he could only go on what he knew. He knew he had to find her. Despite the trouble that could come from it, he had to talk to her again.

Sapphire stood by the side of the road and watched the floats go by. There weren't many times in her life where she was taken over by anything that felt good. It was usually the bad that filled her head. But she decided that she was going to feel good right now, in the moment. She spent most of her time every day blaming herself for everything and anything. Today, while she was here, surrounded by happiness, she was going to take a bit of it for herself. Just for a bit. She closed her eyes, and finally, she let go. She started to move with the music.

Sapphire had only been dancing for about three seconds before she felt a pair of hands snake around her waist.

'No,' she said, turning round. 'No.'

She came face to face with a tall, blonde man who was clearly a few years older than her.

'What do you mean, no?' the guy said. 'For God's sake, loosen up!'

'I don't need to loosen up, just don't touch me please,' Sapphire said, stepping out of his grip.

She turned back around to face the action and kept her eyes very much open. A dancing woman dressed in full Carnival wear, much like the one Apollo had pointed out by the tube station, smiled and waved at her.

Apollo. Sapphire turned his name around in her head. One of the Gold Teeth. One of nine men in the whole of London she definitely shouldn't think about, let alone have spoken to. Let alone have kissed.

Sapphire carried on dancing and waving back until the float passed. When it did, she felt arms move around her waist again. She turned around and looked at the same blonde man.

'Babe, just go with it, yeah?' he said, smiling and slurring his words a little.

'I don't want to go with it!' Sapphire shouted, pushing the man away. 'I want you to get off my body!'

'Calm down, girly!' A bearded man, who was clearly a friend of the blonde man, stood in front of her so that Sapphire was sandwiched in by both of them.

She could feel anger bubbling in her. She took a deep breath. If she said that she had to go and meet a friend, she could just walk away without making a scene. Sapphire had learnt not to make a scene.

'Excuse me guys, my friends are over there,' Sapphire said, trying to move sideways away from them.

'Your friends can wait,' the bearded man said, moving closer to Sapphire so that he and his blonde friend pressed her in between them tightly.

Sapphire went to shout, and took a deep breath at the same time that the bearded man laughed in her face, his horrible beer breath filling her nostrils.

She coughed, like she was trying to stop the smell from going down to her stomach.

'Come on, dance for us!' Sapphire heard the blonde man say, while his friend laughed.

Sapphire felt heat rising from her feet. 'Don't make a scene, don't make a scene,' she said over and over to herself.

She closed her eyes tightly as they pushed closer into her, hoping it would end soon.

Suddenly, Sapphire could breathe again. She opened her eyes and the bearded man was in front of her on the floor.

She turned behind her to see what had happened and saw Apollo behind the blonde man. Apollo was holding him tightly by the scruff of the neck, even though he was much shorter than him.

Apollo threw the blonde man on the floor next to his bearded friend.

'Apologise to my friend,' Apollo said.

'We were only joking, mate!' the bearded man said, holding his hands up.

'No you weren't,' Apollo said. 'It's not a joke unless everyone can laugh at it. And my friend wasn't laughing.'

'I hear what you're saying, but we meant no harm,' the blonde man said.

'But what you did was harmful to my friend,' Apollo said. Then he turned to Sapphire. 'Have you got anything to say to them?'

'If a girl tells you to let her go, let her go,' Sapphire said. 'In fact! Don't even touch her!'

'Is that all?' Apollo asked her.

'Yes. Thank you,' Sapphire said. She didn't want to get too angry in front of him. She was already waiting for him to run away from her after what he'd heard earlier. If anything, she was surprised to see him again.

They both walked away, Sapphire shaking a little bit, and didn't stop until they found a wall to sit on.

'You all right, yeah?' Apollo asked Sapphire.

'Yeah. You?' She laughed, squinting and putting a hand up to shield her eyes from the sun. 'Thanks for that. I don't think I've ever been rescued before.'

'So,' Apollo said.

'So,' Sapphire said. 'You heard the cell thing, didn't you?'

'That's the thing you're worried about?' Apollo laughed.

They turned to face each other. Sapphire took her hand away from her face and Apollo held it. Then he held the other.

'This isn't going to end well,' Sapphire said as Apollo moved closer to her.

'We don't need to think about endings now,' Apollo said as he kissed her softly.

Chapter Six

'Come in, take your shoes off,' Sapphire said to Apollo.

'Obviously.' He smiled, kicking his trainers off.

'It's not much, but it's mine. Ish.' Sapphire gestured to the small studio room that contained all of her worldly possessions. Everything she had, not the stuff that had been provided by her landlord, was a few outfits, two pairs of black trainers, a second-hand laptop and a pair of speakers.

'Oh, and there's a little garden,' Sapphire said. 'We all have to share it, but my neighbours are cool.'

'Your flat is very clean,' Apollo said, thinking that it was the most empty room he'd ever stepped foot in. One bed, one bedside table, one lamp, one chest of drawers and one small battered sofa.

'Apollo,' Sapphire laughed. 'Stop looking around and have a seat. Want a drink? I'm so dehydrated.'

They'd spent the rest of the day dancing until the sun went down. Then they carried on as it got darker. They'd barely spoken because it was just enough being together, but had lost track of time, again.

'Me too. Water's good, thanks,' Apollo said, lowering himself onto the sofa. He was too young for his knees to be creaking like this, he thought.

Sapphire walked over to the kitchen area as Apollo looked around slowly. He thought about buying her a poster.

'You cook much?' Apollo asked.

'A bit,' Sapphire said over her shoulder. 'You?'

'Yeah,' Apollo told her. 'I'm not elite, but I can cook.'

'I'm far from elite. Here you go.' Sapphire came over to the sofa, two glasses of water in hand. They sat side by side and took quiet sips. Next thing they knew, they'd dozed off.

An hour or so later, Apollo woke up slowly. Realising where he was, he turned to look at Sapphire, and smiled when he saw her sleeping face. Her eyeliner was smudged and her bronzer was marked with sweat lines. She was so beautiful, he thought. She looked so peaceful.

'I know you're looking at me,' Sapphire said

sleepily, her eyes still closed. 'Like when you thought I couldn't see you staring at me on the tube.'

Apollo chuckled to himself. 'I thought I was being discreet on the tube.'

'Not even nearly,' Sapphire laughed, opening her eyes. 'From the minute you "accidentally" fell on me.'

'That *was* an accident, I swear,' Apollo assured her. 'Wait – so even when I came and spoke to you at Oxford Circus you knew I'd been watching? Is that why you ran away?'

'I only ran away because I thought all our peoples were going to end up on the news!' Sapphire told him. 'Plus I didn't know you.'

'Shall we talk about stuff?' Apollo said.

'Which stuff?' Sapphire asked him, sitting up. She knew he'd bring up the prison stuff. No time like the present, she thought, gulping. She took a sip of water.

'Seriously?' Apollo said, cocking his head to look at her.

'Look,' Sapphire started. 'I was young – not that young, I guess. I was almost eighteen. But I got too involved in that stupid gang shit, got carried away, wanted to show everyone I was big and bad, and ended up really hurting someone.'

Sapphire paused to cross her legs. She looked into her lap before speaking again. 'You know, I regret it every single day. That's why I'm trying to get everyone to realise that these stupid actions can have serious outcomes.'

Apollo put a hand on Sapphire's knee.

'I tried to reach out to Ricky, you know,' she said quietly. 'I wrote him a letter. He never replied. Why should he though?'

'We all do stupid shit,' Apollo said. 'I didn't even mean the prison stuff. We all have past shit. I meant we should talk about the fact that I'm in the Gold Teeth.'

'Oh!' Sapphire said. 'Why didn't you stop me from talking?'

'Why would I stop you?' Apollo asked. 'You were talking about something important to you. Plus, I like watching you talk. You're very full of feeling, you know.'

Sapphire laughed, again. She hadn't properly laughed for ages. She turned to look at Apollo, almost to try and understand him. Who was this boy? Why did they have this connection? What was it that made her want to tell him everything about her, even the bad stuff? *Especially* the bad stuff? And why did he have to be one of the worst people to fall for? There was a feeling in Sapphire's chest that she couldn't understand. She hadn't felt it before. It didn't feel . . . comfortable. It felt too alien.

'What are you thinking about?' Apollo asked, stroking Sapphire's face.

'Nothing,' she said.

'Not true,' Apollo told her.

'This ain't realistic. Me and you,' Sapphire said. 'It can't carry on.'

'Yes it can,' Apollo said. 'We just need to figure it out. We might need to just be, like, discreet with it.'

Sapphire shook her head. Even if both gangs called a truce this evening, it would take a long time for them to be acceptable. Plus she wasn't even confident about this truce business. It worried her – how easy it was for Pinky and Zora to agree to chat. Especially knowing what Den was like. Always loved the chaos, always looking to start trouble, even if it wasn't his own.

'You know what,' Sapphire said. 'I don't think they're going to call a truce at all.'

'You might be right,' Apollo agreed.

Sapphire suddenly froze. 'What time is it?'

'I dunno. I left my phone at home, haven't had it all day,' Apollo said.

Sapphire jumped up and ran over to the kitchen counter. 'It's just after 1 a.m.!'

57

'We've been chatting for ages.' Apollo smiled. 'Didn't even notice.'

'We were meant to be at Dawn's at midnight!' Sapphire yelped, running to the door and pulling her trainers on. 'Come on!'

Apollo jumped up and followed her, stuffing his feet into his trainers and pulling his jacket on.

They ran down the road, dodging people spilling out into the street from the bars and pubs. People who were actually enjoying their bank holiday weekend.

Drawing closer to the café, they slowed down.

'Aren't you cold? You left your jumper at yours,' Apollo said.

'I'm fine!' Sapphire told him.

'Why don't you take my jacket?'

'What kind of war are you trying to start?' Sapphire asked, turning to look at him.

'I just want you to be warm!' Apollo said, holding her hand.

'You should hang back a bit,' Sapphire said. The café was a few steps away and they could already hear heated voices.

'What do we have here?' Den's voice came from the shadows before he did. 'Apollo's plucked himself a Red Rose, yeah?'

Sapphire pulled her hand free from Apollo's, obviously too late.

'You know what they say about roses innit?' Den snarled.

'If you're going to say something about being pricked by thorns or something, please miss me with that.' Sapphire rolled her eyes.

'The fuck is this?' Pinky asked, shaking her head as she walked over. 'How long has *this* been happening? This is why you want us to have a *truce*? Because you're linking Zora's *twin*?'

'Apollo, have you lost your fucking head?' Zora shouted, falling in line with Den and Pinky. This was the first time the three of them had ever agreed on anything.

'You lot know this can't go on,' Apollo spoke, his heart beating fast but his voice steady. 'And yeah? So what? We like each other.'

Sapphire's heart was beating fast too, but when she heard him say that, it felt very full.

'I should have been leader from the beginning,' Pinky snarled, stepping closer to Sapphire and pointing a red-tipped finger in her face.

Pinky was the angriest she'd been in a long time.

'Pinky, leave it,' Kyla said, more scared for Pinky than she was for her sister.

'Listen,' Sapphire said, swiping Pinky's hand out of her face in one move. 'I don't know where you got this vim and chest from, but

I am ready to end you, you know. You know how patient I've been with you?'

'Patient with *me*?' Pinky laughed. 'You think this gang is yours? Girls, a show of hands if *I'm* your leader.'

One by one, all of the Red Roses, including Sapphire's sister Kyla, raised their hands.

'Even you, Kyla?' Sapphire said. 'I see how it is.'

'You don't want this life!' Kyla said. 'You left it behind and for a good reason, sis.'

'Oh shit, if we wait here long enough the Red Roses are going to destroy themselves,' Den laughed.

Pinky turned to face him and sneered. 'How many fights have *you* been in, Den? Me and aaall your boys know you let everyone else do your dirty work. Never on the frontline, are you?'

Some of the Gold Teeth sniggered until Den looked around at them, making a mental note of who found it funny. There was a lot of crew betrayal going on.

'I'm gone,' Sapphire said. 'Let me leave you lot to do what you're doing. I can't get pulled back in.'

Sapphire turned and walked away. She both did and didn't want Apollo to follow her. He stayed where he was, knowing that him walking away with her would be bad news for them both. He also knew he had to get involved in what was to come somehow.

'Look, I'm done with this nonsense,' Pinky said. 'Our best fighter versus yours, tomorrow.'

'Where and when?' Den said. 'Give the time and place and let's go.'

'Not round here,' Pinky said. 'You know that green in the middle of Carnival? Powis Square? There.'

'That's dumb,' Leon said. 'In the *middle* of everything? You tryna arrange suttin? Is this some sort of set-up?'

'Nah, think about it. Police won't be in the busy *park*, they'll be on the streets, and by the time they get to us it'll be done.'

'She's right,' Zora said.

Den held a hand up to silence Zora, and thought about it for a second. Pinky was right in some ways; the fight would be over in seconds. He was certain that they'd win it. Plus, it was better to do it off ends. If they all had to scatter it would be easier to hide in the crowds.

'What time?' Den asked.

'When it's busiest,' Pinky said. 'Three p.m.'

Pinky went to walk away and cocked her head, summoning the rest of the Red Roses to follow her.

61

'One thing,' Apollo said, stepping forwards. 'No weapons.'

'Fine,' Zora agreed, smiling.

'Fine. Get ready, Zora,' Pinky smiled back as she crossed the road, her girls following her like little red ducks in a line.

Sapphire settled into bed and for a good hour she lay there, looking at the ceiling and thinking hard. She shouldn't have left so soon, she should have stayed and sorted it. If things carried on as she predicted, it was all going to end very badly for everyone involved. It wasn't only that she didn't want her sister involved; it was what this whole thing would say to their communities.

The Red Roses and the Gold Teeth had a chance to turn things around, to stop all this mess, to put everything behind them. Sapphire also felt guilty. She couldn't get rid of the feeling, the knowledge, that she'd started all of this years ago.

She sat up with a start as she heard a small knock on the window. She was on the first floor, so put it down to a tree branch. She lay back down and closed her eyes. *Knock knock* again.

She got out of bed and crept over to the window, peeling the curtain back slowly. Apollo.

Sapphire opened the window and watched him tumble in and land on the floor.

'Take your shoes off please.'

'I've scaled your building and that's the first thing you say to me?' Apollo laughed, standing up.

'What happened?' she asked him, not laughing.

'I came to tell you,' Apollo began. 'They've agreed to have one fight, Zora and Pinky. Then it's done.'

'Can't you see that it won't be done as long as it begins with a fight?' Sapphire asked him. 'And what about your sister? Don't you care about her getting hurt?'

'My sister could take me three times over,' Apollo said. 'But look, they've agreed to no weapons. Which is good, right?'

'Who agreed?' Sapphire asked him.

'Zora and Pinky.'

'Lies.' Sapphire shook her head. 'They're both liars. Weapons will be brought, trust me.'

'If I know my sister, she might bring one, but she won't use it.' Apollo shrugged. 'And if she won't, Pinky won't either. But look, I don't think we should go. Me and you. It just complicates things.'

'Apollo, you're being naive. I have to go there,' Sapphire said. 'Properly stop it.'

'But what's the point?' Apollo asked her. 'I don't want you getting hurt.'

'Listen,' Sapphire said. 'You haven't seen me fight. And why are you more worried about me than your sister?'

'You think too much innit. Let's talk about this in the morning,' Apollo said. 'For tonight, let's just sleep.'

Chapter Seven

The next day, Bank Holiday Monday, the sun shone bright and hard. The rain of yesterday was forgotten. As the Red Roses and the Gold Teeth approached the park from opposite sides, sounds of enjoyment and happiness ringing around west London could be heard.

Dancing, laughter, whistles, horns, the faint thud of various songs from various sound systems being carried through the air.

It was all about to darken.

As Pinky walked towards the meeting point, she could feel her stomach churn. She knew that if this went her way, nobody would ever be able to doubt her again. She also knew, from years of watching her fight, that as strong as Zora was, Pinky was quicker.

Zora felt completely calm and still. All she was thinking about was how strong she was, and how good it was that Den had finally let her have her chance in the limelight.

The Red Roses stood on one side, forming a semicircle, and the Gold Teeth went on the other side, completing the circle. Two members of each crew were tasked with watching for the police from different angles of the circle.

'Go on, Zora. Show us what you're made of, innit,' Den said, squeezing Zora's shoulder roughly.

Zora looked around for her brother. Why wasn't he there? A burst of anger directed at Sapphire propelled Zora into the middle of the circle, and Pinky followed.

'Hope you're ready to never be able to show face again,' Zora snarled, throwing her fists up.

'You're doing a lot of talking when you could be fighting, Zora,' Pinky said, stretching from side to side.

Zora jumped towards Pinky, throwing the first jab, which Pinky avoided with ease. Years of gymnastics in her younger days meant that she was very agile.

Pinky responded with a quick hit to Zora's stomach, which didn't do the job of winding her that Pinky thought it would.

'Come on girls!' Den shouted. 'I've seen little kids who fight better than this!' He wanted to see blood.

Riled up by Den, Zora threw an upper cut that connected with Pinky's jaw. Pinky stumbled back and clutched the side of her face.

Zora came towards her again so Pinky lifted her leg and delivered a kick that connected hard with Zora's groin.

'Oh shit!' Den laughed as Zora doubled over. 'Now we're talking!'

'Stop stop stop!' Sapphire cried, pushing her way into the circle. 'Stop! Look around you!'

Pinky, still holding her jaw, looked outside of the circle, while Zora, her groin starting to throb with pain, did the same. Hundreds of people were watching, most holding their phones up to record what was going on.

'Didn't I tell you this would happen?' Sapphire shouted. 'All of this is already on socials! People don't *rate* you, they're laughing at you!'

'Stay out of it, Sapphire man!' Pinky shouted. 'I've got her!'

'At least they're going to remember me!' Zora shouted. 'Unlike you, Sapphire! You'll be forgotten. Not by Ricky, obviously. He'll always remember you.'

'That was an accident!' Sapphire shouted, looking around the circle. 'And I'm sorry!'

'Don't matter if you're sorry or not!' Zora snarled. 'Ricky can't even leave the house. He thinks everyone is laughing at him.'

Sapphire's breathing started to quicken. 'I tried to apologise.'

'What's an apology when you ruined someone's life?' Zora shouted. 'He's only twenty.'

'Why are you throwing this in my face?' Sapphire felt like her chest was on fire. She tried to hold it down. She came here to stop a fight, not start one.

Kyla gripped her girlfriend Katrina's hand. She was worried for her sister. She was starting to see the Sapphire that she'd thought, and hoped, was dead and buried.

'Ah, that's it!' Zora laughed. 'I see the old Sapphire is coming out! Yes!'

'Oh, you don't want the old Sapphire,' Sapphire growled.

'Why don't we want the old Sapphire?' Zora asked. 'The old Sapphire was so much fun! The old Sapphire was crazy. Crazy, crazy, CRAZY!'

'Don't!' Kyla shouted as her fist connected with Zora's nose. 'Don't talk about my sister like that!'

Zora stumbled back, blood dripping onto her top lip.

'You know what happens when the rules get broken, don't you, Kyla?' she asked, ignoring the blood.

'Oh, Kyla,' Sapphire groaned. 'You shouldn't have done that.'

'We can break the rules too,' Zora said, pulling a large silver kitchen knife from the inside of her jacket.

'Fuck's sake!' Sapphire shouted, the rate of her already pounding heart getting even faster.

'Come then!' Pinky shouted, reaching into the back of her tracksuit bottoms where she'd concealed a small flip knife. She pulled it out and flicked it open.

'Do something!' Sapphire shouted to Den.

'It's out of my hands.' Den smiled, licking his lips. He was finally going to get the blood he wanted.

Pinky jumped towards Zora clumsily, jabbing the knife towards her, but Zora swerved out of the way and sliced the kitchen knife across Pinky's arm. Pinky cried out and dropped her knife.

Sapphire knew that it was all happening so fast, but felt like it was happening in slow motion. She felt frozen to the spot.

Pinky went to pick her knife back up but was floored by a kick from Zora, who threw herself on top of her, pinning Pinky to the floor. Pinky went to reach for her knife, her hand scrambling across the grass. But she stopped and closed her eyes when she saw the glint of Zora's knife coming down towards her.

Sapphire finally came unstuck and lunged for Zora, pulling her off Pinky. Zora turned to face Sapphire, the wild expression on her face terrifying.

Sapphire used all of her strength and pushed Zora away from her, hard. She watched her fall and land heavily on her side.

'Get up, Pinky!' Sapphire commanded. 'And put that away.'

Pinky did as she was told, finally finding the flip knife, folding it down and putting it in her pocket.

'Get up, Zora!' Sapphire shouted. 'This is done, you hear me? This is done!'

Zora didn't get up.

'Get up, Zora!' Den shouted, embarrassed as he walked over to his second-in-command.

Zora still didn't get up.

'Oi, let's just go, Z.' Den shook his head. He was annoyed that he'd let the girls run things. All this drama, and nothing had happened.

Den went over to Zora and held out his hand to pull her up.

'Z?' Den suddenly yelped, startled. 'There's blood!'

Sapphire felt all of the heat leave her body, and her blood ran as cold as ice. She watched Den turn Zora over. Zora had fallen on her knife, and blood was trickling from her side. Her eyes were closed.

'Someone call an ambulance!' Den shouted. 'Fuck! Someone call an ambulance!'

Everyone in the circle, whether they were wearing red rose patterned tops or blue and gold Nike windbreakers, got their phones out and called 999. Their voices and their shock all blurred into the same panicked mass of noise.

'Is she still alive?' Sapphire asked, going to Zora, kneeling next to her to take her pulse.

'Get the *fuck* off her,' Den growled, shoving Sapphire away. 'This is your fault.'

'My fault?' Sapphire shouted at him. 'You were the one who wanted this!'

For the first time in his life, Den felt guilt. Even after what happened with Ricky, after years of nothing more than punches and kicks, he had never thought it would come to this.

'Den,' Sapphire pleaded with him. 'Let me at least check!'

The noise of sirens filled the air.

'Sis,' Kyla said. 'You've got to go.'

'No!' Sapphire said. 'I've got to stay, I should explain.'

'Sapphire! They aren't going to listen to you.' Kyla grabbed her sister by the shoulders. 'Run. Go.'

Sapphire ran. She ran as fast as her legs could carry her, pushing her way through bodies at full pelt, and didn't stop running until she got to the tube station. She jumped over the barriers and ran down the stairs, falling into the tube carriage and throwing herself onto a seat before her legs gave way.

Sapphire panted hard, putting her head between her knees until she was sure she wasn't going to faint. When she looked up, her carriage was almost empty. She inspected herself and felt like she'd faint again when she saw some of Zora's blood that had dried on her jumper.

She took it off and folded it up. Where was she going to go? What was she going to do? *I should have stayed*, she thought on a loop. At least if she'd have stayed she could have explained. By running she looked like she'd done something. Well, she *had* done something, but this way she looked like she'd done something intentionally.

Sapphire changed tube lines and headed to Brixton. She didn't want to head home while it was light out, in case the police were on her case. She decided that she'd slip into the back of Dawn's café and hide out in the stock room until Dawn closed up. It was like a fortress in there, with a very dim light so that she could stay in the shadows but also not fall over when she needed to move.

Most of the Red Roses and the Gold Teeth travelled back to south London together. Nobody was talking, but their silence said the words of regret that they couldn't find yet.

Pinky had run away seconds after Sapphire had, to get rid of her knife, and Den had ridden in the ambulance, when it had finally turned up, with an unconscious Zora.

When they got back to Brixton, some were crying, others were shaking. They all scattered silently, nodding their goodbyes.

'Den?' Apollo answered his phone quickly. He'd gone straight to his house, expecting to hear from Sapphire, not from Den. 'What you saying? . . . What? Man, speak clearly! What? . . . Which hospital? . . . I'll be there soon.'

Apollo ran down the stairs and into the kitchen, where he found his dad looking in the fridge and swaying gently to Beres Hammond. He paused before speaking, trying to make sense of what he was about to tell his dad. His head was spinning and he felt kind of sick.

'Dad,' he finally said over the music. 'Get your shoes on, we need to go to the hospital.'

'What was that?' Glen asked, turning the radio down. 'You and your sister are always interrupting me when I'm trying to relax!'

'Dad, we need to go to the hospital,' Apollo repeated. 'It's Zora.'

Chapter Eight

Apollo and Glen sat on either side of Zora, who was no longer in a critical condition, but still hadn't woken up.

Glen checked his watch. It was 9 p.m. 'You must be starving. You eaten?' he asked his son.

Apollo shook his head.

'You know, I thought it was you who'd end up in the hospital bed, not your sister,' Glen said slowly, running a hand across his smooth bald head.

'Why?' Apollo asked.

'Because you're a boy,' Glen told him, taking a small sip of his weak vending machine coffee. 'You boys are always in that ruckus.'

'You don't know either of us at all, then,' Apollo sighed. 'Have you called Mum?'

'No,' Glen said, putting his head in his hands. 'What's she going to do?'

'She's got a right to know, Dad,' Apollo said, getting up from the hard plastic chair and stretching. 'I'm going to call her.'

Apollo walked out of the ward to get some

fresh air. He took his phone out of his pocket and saw that he had two missed calls from a number he didn't know. He called back, knowing who would be on the other end of the line.

'I don't know what they've told you, but it was an accident, Apollo,' Sapphire whispered down the line as soon as he picked up. 'I am so, so sorry. Is she OK?'

'I'm not sure,' Apollo told her. He couldn't speak to her right now. He needed to get his head in check. 'Got to go.' He ended the call.

Apollo searched through his phone for his mum's number. She was living across the city with her new husband and their baby daughter. He sighed from his feet to his chest. It was going to be a long night.

Sapphire paced up and down in the stock room of the café to keep alert. She'd been in there for ages. She could hear people laughing and eating while she wanted to tear her hair out. Poor Zora, Sapphire thought, her stomach tying itself in more knots. Sapphire hated the idea of Zora being hurt. So much chaos, and actual bloodshed and over what? She closed her eyes and wished that Zora would be OK. And Apollo! Apollo hated her, surely he hated her. It was an accident, but she'd definitely just messed her life up completely, and why? She'd worked so long and so hard at being able to stop that red mist before it took her over. But Zora was right, she was always going to be the old Sapphire. That hot-headed girl who didn't know how to control herself when things got on top of her.

Sapphire couldn't stop her thoughts from whirring around her head. Her mind was going into complete overdrive when she heard someone outside the stock room door, and ducked down behind a giant sack of potatoes. She heard the door open slowly and held her breath. She closed her eyes, only opening them and exhaling when she heard the door close.

'Sapphire?' Kyla whispered. 'You here?'

'I'm here,' Sapphire replied quietly. 'How's Zora?'

'I've been calling you,' Kyla said. 'She's going to be OK, we think. It's not critical.'

'Oh, thank God.' Sapphire exhaled, relief filling her.

Kyla squinted in the dim light, found Sapphire and walked over to her. She sat next to her on the cold stone floor.

'It's quite nice sitting in here when it's so hot outside,' Kyla said.

Sapphire let out a small laugh, one that very quickly turned to tears.

'Does Mum know? Is it on the news?' she asked, trying not to sob.

'Mum doesn't need to know anything. As far as she knows we're having a nice time at Carnival,' Kyla said, wiping the tears from her sister's face.

Kyla put her arm around her big sister and leant her head on Sapphire's shoulder. 'It's going to be OK.'

'Is it?' Sapphire asked, wiping tears away with the back of her hand.

'I think so?' Kyla said. 'We all got the tube home together and kind of said goodbye. That's a start, isn't it?'

'Really?' Sapphire said. 'Well at least something good has come out of all this madness. Not sure about Den, though. He's not going to let it drop. Or Zora.'

'They aren't anything without their crew. Oh! Nobody said anything to the police, by the way,' Kyla said. 'Sorry, should probably have said that at the beginning. By the time them stupid officers got to us, Pinky was gone and we all said Zora fell on her knife.'

'And they believed you?' Sapphire asked.

'Well it's true,' Kyla told her, putting her free hand on Sapphire's knee. 'And all those dumb people filming it is evidence of that.'

Sapphire let out a big sigh.

'Why don't you come home to Mum's?' Kyla asked. 'Me, you and Mum, the gang all back together. She hasn't seen you for ages. It'll make her happy.'

'I'm still going to lie low for a bit,' Sapphire said. 'And I don't want to bring police to her door *again*. She still hasn't forgiven me for the last time, I can tell.'

'Sis. Of course she's forgiven you.' Kyla rolled her eyes. 'And police aren't coming to anyone's doors, I'm telling you.'

'Just until early hours,' Sapphire said. 'When the café is closed and the streets are quiet I'll go home.'

'Suit yourself,' Kyla said. 'I'll call you if I hear anything about Zora.'

'Cool. My battery's dead, but I'll charge my phone when I get home,' Sapphire said. 'Kyla?'

Kyla turned to look at her sister.

'Do you think Apollo hates me?'

Kyla didn't have an answer. If anyone on the planet had even *nearly* caused her sister to be hurt, she'd definitely hate them. But this was different.

'I think you need to talk to him,' Kyla eventually said.

'Can you let him know I'm here?' Sapphire asked. 'If you see him.'

'Of course,' Kyla said, letting herself out of the stock room and closing the door behind her.

Sapphire laid her head against the sack of potatoes and closed her eyes. Mentally and physically, she was exhausted.

Kyla walked up the hill towards her house, still hot and a bit shaken up from earlier. She still hadn't seen or heard from Pinky, and wondered if she was OK after taking such a beating. She was going to be livid. When she got to the end of her road, she met Katrina, who'd been waiting patiently for her.

'Was she there?' Katrina asked, taking a seat on the wall.

Kyla nodded, sitting next to her. 'I don't know what she's in that stock room for. Or how Dawn hasn't caught her.'

'Your poor sister.' Katrina sighed. 'It's like the worst kind of trouble follows her round. I don't know anyone as unlucky as her, you know.'

Kyla thought she could see someone lurking round the corner, so she jumped up. She'd been in the Red Roses long enough to always be alert.

'What?' Katrina asked.

'Thought someone was lurking,' Kyla said, shaking her head. She was exhausted and thought she was seeing things. 'Ignore me.'

'Did you tell her we all said it was an accident?' Katrina checked.

'Yeah, but I think she's convinced that she's going to get in trouble because she's got priors,' Kyla told her.

'We shouldn't be talking about this here,' Katrina said, looking behind her.

Den walked away from the end of the road. He'd heard all he needed to.

Zora woke up, her eyes blurry as she looked around the room and tried to take in her surroundings. She looked to her left and saw her brother sleeping, somehow propped up in what looked like an uncomfortable plastic chair. Zora went to say his name, but she couldn't speak yet.

'Zora!' she heard her dad say. 'You're awake.'

The sound of his sister's name woke Apollo too.

'Z!' Apollo said. 'How you feeling?'

Zora managed the best smile she could, nodding a little to show that she felt at least all right.

'Go and get the nurse!' Glen said to Apollo.

Apollo did as he was told, and as he left the room, bumped into Den, holding a small bottle of orange Lucozade. For himself.

'Bro,' Apollo said. 'Good to see you.'

81

'It's the opp,' Den said, shaking his head. 'Surprised you aren't with your little Red Rose.'

'Den, man,' Apollo started. 'Isn't this done now?'

'How can this be done?' Den hissed. 'Monday isn't even done, how can *this* be over?'

'Excuse me, boys,' a nurse said firmly, stopping as she walked past them. 'Please can you take any arguments outside? There are a lot of poorly people in here that you're disturbing.'

'Sorry ma'am.' Den flashed a smile until she carried on walking. As soon as she was out of sight, his smile dropped.

'Listen man, you know I wouldn't just fall for any and any girl,' Apollo said. 'Sapphire is special.'

'Sapphire almost killed your sister,' Den told him. 'This is exactly what happens when you consort with the enemy.'

'The enemy?' Apollo laughed. 'Z fell on the knife *she* brought to a fight you were fully backing, Den! A fight you wanted because your ego is still stuck in Year Nine! This is all school shit gone too far. Sapphire isn't even in all of that any more.'

'How can you laugh?' Den asked Apollo. 'You wouldn't be laughing if the ambulance hadn't come in time.'

'I'm laughing because you're talking like we're in some film!' Apollo said. 'And look, the ambulance did come on time. We don't need to be doing what ifs. I met Sapphire and I fell for her, man, I can't think about what if I hadn't met her either. I did, and that's where we are now. What happened was an accident, and it happened because you lot want to carry on like it's a war out there. Sapphire only stepped in because she wanted to stop it all.'

Den screwed up his face as he listened to his boy. 'So you're telling me you and her is gonna carry on?' he asked. His mouth was so tight with anger he could barely get the words out.

'Yeah, man.' Apollo sighed. 'That's exactly what I'm telling you.'

'If you and her carry on, you're out of the Gold Teeth, you know that innit?' Den snarled.

'Yeah, and my sister will be out too by the looks of things. And if she's gone her boy Francis is gone, and if he's gone then his best mate Leon has gone. So where does that leave you?' Apollo asked.

Den stopped for a second. He had to play this properly.

'Well, look. I hate to be the one to break it to you,' Den said, looking Apollo dead in the eye, 'but your girl Sapphire has gone. Fled.

Bumped into her sister a couple hours ago and she told me.'

'What?' Apollo snorted. 'Gone where?'

'I dunno. Her sister was crying and saying Sapphire was scared, so had gone to stay with some family in the country for the foreseeable.'

'Nah. She wouldn't.' Apollo shook his head.

'How do you know?' Den asked. 'You don't know her, bro. You met her *yesterday*. You don't know anything about her.'

Maybe Den was right, Apollo thought. The past twenty-four hours had meant a lot to him, but maybe they meant nothing to her.

'Surely she'd have said goodbye to me,' Apollo said to himself.

'I heard it from her sister, man.' Den shrugged. 'She bounced this afternoon, straight from West.'

Apollo's heart sank to his knees. He'd only spoken to her a few hours ago. Wouldn't she have told him when they spoke? Maybe she wanted to tell him before he put the phone down.

Without saying another word, Apollo ran from the ward. He sat on the bus back to Brixton calling Sapphire's phone constantly. It kept going to voicemail. Why didn't he tell her it was all OK earlier? He was so angry with himself.

When he finally got back to South, he ran all the way to Sapphire's house. He rang the bell until one of her neighbours came down and said he hadn't seen her since the morning. Apollo scaled the outside wall again, the same way he did the night before, and peered through the window. No sign of her. The flat was exactly as it was when they'd left that morning. Cups on the side, bed unmade.

He made his way to Dawn's café. When he got there, hot and very bothered, he ran up to the counter and asked Dawn if she'd seen Sapphire.

'Not seen or heard from her since her shift on Saturday,' Dawn said, wiping the side down. 'She in trouble?'

'No, nothing like that,' Apollo said, racking his brains. Where else could she be? Was it true she'd just left?

Apollo headed back home. He was exhausted and his head was spinning. When he got in, he sat on the sofa and tried calling Sapphire from the house phone in case she'd blocked his mobile. Voicemail again. He looked at the clock on the wall, ticking away loudly. It was just before ten and was finally getting dark. He closed his eyes for a second, and just one second later, Apollo was asleep.

*

Sapphire woke up in pain. Sleeping next to a sack of potatoes on a cold stone floor was not the one. She stood up slowly, wondering what time it was. She wished that the stock room had at least a small window so that she could see if it was dark yet.

She went to the door and listened before cracking it open. Silence. She opened it slowly and saw nothing but darkness.

Sapphire crept out into the hallway and into the shop. She turned a lamp on and looked at the clock on the wall. It was almost midnight. When would this bank holiday weekend *end*?

She scrambled around the counter to see if she could find a charger to plug her phone in, but found nothing. Surely it was late enough to head back home?

A small knock on the door of the café startled her.

'I know you're in there,' Den said through the letterbox. 'I'm not here for trouble, I swear.'

Sapphire grabbed the spare keys and walked over to the door, opening it slowly.

'You heard about Zora?' Den asked, stepping into the shop.

'Yeah,' Sapphire said. 'She's gonna be OK, right?'

'She was taken to intensive care,' Den lied. 'We don't know what's gonna happen.'

'Fuck,' Sapphire exhaled. 'Is Apollo OK?'

'Nah, I don't think so,' Den said, pulling up a chair and taking a seat. 'But look, I came to warn you.'

'Warn me about what?' Sapphire asked, fear spiking through her.

'Apollo's looking for you,' Den said. 'He's out for you.'

'What?' Sapphire asked, her voice beginning to tremble. 'But I spoke to him earlier? He knows it was an accident!'

'Yeah, but the thing is, Sapphire, Zora's his twin, innit. No one, especially not a girl, is ever gonna come between him and his blood. You must know that.'

Sapphire felt her stomach churn.

'I know you don't know him well,' Den said. 'Apollo was never about when we were growing up. Went to the posh school. He's a smart guy.'

Sapphire was so shaken that she struggled to listen to what Den was saying.

'A very smart guy. If I were you, I wouldn't want to run into him when he's like this. I can't imagine how he's going to get revenge. *Whatever* you think you and him have,' Den said quietly, 'if I were you, I'd run.'

'Run where?' Sapphire asked. 'I don't have anywhere to go!'

Den shrugged. 'Well. If his sister dies tonight, you better find somewhere to go.'

Sapphire sat down on the table. Her legs weren't going to hold her up much longer.

'Anyway,' Den said, standing up. 'Just came to let you know.'

'Den,' Sapphire said. 'If I go, can you promise all this stuff stops?'

Den looked at her. 'Yeah. I can promise that. We're all getting too old for these games.'

Sapphire let Den out and locked the door behind him. She had nowhere to go. Not one place to go. Her mum wasn't going to let her stay at theirs, not with this going on. She had no other family in another part of London, or even England. She had some family in Jamaica she hadn't seen for ages, but she didn't have any money to get there. She could take money from Dawn's, but she would never, ever do that. Ever.

There was only one thing for it, she thought.

Apollo was out on the streets again, searching for Sapphire. He walked past Dawn's café again and thought he saw a light on, but was distracted when Pinky called to him from across the road. She hadn't gone home yet. She was still rattled from the day's events.

'How's your sister?' she asked.

'She's awake,' Apollo told her. 'I spoke to my dad an hour ago and she's talking. Still a bit out of it and in pain, but she's OK.'

'Listen,' Pinky said. 'I know I'm a hothead, but I'm sorry it went down like that. I only brought the knife to protect myself. I didn't plan to use it.'

'Yeah, but that's how these things happen, innit,' Apollo said. 'You think you aren't going to do anything, but you get scared and then look where we are.'

Sapphire left Dawn's café, and what she saw across the road made her heart stop. There Apollo was across the road, talking to Pinky. He was definitely looking for her. She crept into a corner of darkness that would hide her, and looked over at them. They were deep in conversation, and Apollo looked upset.

Sapphire wanted to weep. How could she have made the only person she'd ever cared about like this be in so much pain?

She moved closer to hear what they were talking about.

'When's the last time you saw her?' Apollo asked Pinky.

'In West, at the park,' Pinky said. 'No one I've spoken to has seen Sapphire all day.'

'OK,' Apollo said, clenching his jaw. 'If you see her, tell her I'm looking for her.'

'Will do,' Pinky said. 'And tell your sister I'm sorry, innit. Didn't mean for it to go that far.'

Apollo nodded and headed towards the high street. He'd try Sapphire's flat again.

'Pinky!' Sapphire whispered from the darkness, as soon as she thought Apollo had left.

Pinky jumped and peered in the direction her name had come from. 'Hello?'

'Has he gone?' Sapphire asked, stepping into the light, but not fully.

'Yeah, he's gone,' Pinky said, rubbing her injured arm. 'Why are you hiding? Where've you been all day?'

'I've been in the stock room,' Sapphire said. 'But it's Apollo, he's after me.'

'Is he?'

'Yeah, Den told me earlier,' Sapphire said frantically. 'Look, if you see my sister, tell her I've gone to turn myself in.'

'What?' Pinky yelped. 'Turn yourself in for what?'

'It's my fault that it happened,' Sapphire said. 'Just like Ricky. When I lose it, bad things happen to people who don't deserve them.'

Pinky looked at Sapphire blankly. This was exactly what she wanted. Sapphire out of the way. But what for? Maybe Sapphire was right. Maybe it was the end of the Red Roses.

'I don't think you should do that,' Pinky said, finally.

'I've made up my mind,' Sapphire said, breaking away from Pinky.

'No!' Pinky called out, grabbing Sapphire's arm tightly.

'Pinky, get off me!' Sapphire said, removing herself with ease. Always the strongest.

Sapphire walked off in the direction of the police station.

'Tell my sister I'm sorry,' she shouted back.

Pinky watched Sapphire walk away. She couldn't let this happen, but didn't know how she could stop her. She got her phone out and called Kyla. No answer. She called Katrina. No answer. Apollo! If she spoke to him, surely she could tell him how sorry Sapphire was and he could talk some sense into her. Pinky took a deep breath, and ran in the direction she had seen Apollo go in.

Chapter Nine

It had been a short walk to the police station. Sapphire stood outside, watching people go past. Brixton was always awake, always alive, even at night. She thought about what she would say, how she would explain what she'd done. They already knew her face anyway. She could probably just walk in there and they'd take her in for something or other.

Sapphire let herself cry for a second. This weekend had been one of the most amazing of her life, despite everything. Sure, she was about to hand herself in for a stabbing she didn't really do. And she was in some way maybe to blame for the loss of a life. Even though she kept reminding herself that it was an accident, Sapphire couldn't cope with the battle of feelings that had taken over. Guilt, fear . . . but also love.

She had never, ever in her life met someone who had made her feel the way Apollo had. He didn't just look at her, he saw her. He didn't just listen to her, he heard her. He made her feel like she mattered. Despite everything she'd told him about her past, the things she'd done, accidental or not, he'd accepted her for who she was. But now he hated her, she thought, and the lightness in her stomach turned to lead. Sapphire walked into the police station.

'Apollo!' Pinky said, catching up to him. 'Apollo!'

'Who you running from?' Apollo asked.

'It's Sapphire . . . you need to know she's sorry.'

'I know she is,' Apollo said, sadness in his voice. 'I wanted to tell her I know, and that it's going to be OK, but she's gone.'

'Where's she gone? I just saw her,' Pinky said, breathlessly.

'What? Den said—' Apollo stopped as he realised what Den had done.

'She's been hiding out in the stock room at Dawn's,' Pinky said quickly. 'But look, she thinks you're after her.'

'What?' Apollo exclaimed.

'Den told her you're after her.'

'That *prick*.' Apollo shook his head. '*He* told *me* she'd gone. Left ends.'

'Well, you need to go fast,' Pinky said. 'She's gone to turn herself in.'

Before she'd even finished her sentence, Apollo broke into a run.

When Apollo arrived at the station, he burst through the doors just in time to see Sapphire being taken to the back by an officer. She turned and looked at him as he entered, fear across her face.

'Sapphire!' he shouted. 'Den was lying!'

'What?' Sapphire shouted back.

'I would never hurt you!' Apollo said. 'I love you!'

'I love you!' Sapphire shouted back as the officer pulled her through the doors.

Apollo stood and watched the doors swinging, tears falling down his face.

One Year Later

'I'm home!' Apollo shouted, kicking off his trainers as he struggled with way too many carrier bags for one person to be carrying.

'You don't need to shout. I'm right here,' Sapphire said, going to him and trying to take some of the bags before kissing him. 'Did you carry all of these up the hill?'

'No, you don't carry anything,' Apollo said. '*You* sit down.'

'Apollo,' Sapphire said. 'I can carry a bit of shopping from the door to the kitchen.'

'The mother of my child cannot do such things,' Apollo smiled, carrying the bags over to the kitchen counter. 'How was your day?'

'If I still have to do my community service, I can carry some milk and bread,' Sapphire said. She went to unload the bags before Apollo swatted her hands away. 'Day was same as usual. How was your day?'

'Good!' Apollo said. 'Dawn's was heaving, as usual. Hiring me as the new chef was the best thing she ever did.'

'And she let you go early?' Sapphire said. 'That was nice of her. She never did that for me, lemme tell you.'

'Baby shower is a good enough reason though, isn't it,' Apollo said. 'Where's Kyla? Thought she was helping you get the garden ready?'

'Go and look!' Sapphire said, putting her earrings in.

Apollo put his sliders on, picked up the carrier bags and went down into the communal garden.

Kyla and Katrina were struggling to erect a balloon arch behind the table that held a huge cake, as well as the empty bowls waiting for the nibbles Apollo had brought home.

'Nice work, Aunty Kyla!' Apollo smiled, fishing crisps out of one of the bags.

'I can't believe you aren't cooking proper food for this,' Kyla said.

'We're about to be parents. I can't afford to be doing big catering for everyone!' Apollo said, pouring the crisps out. 'You didn't want to go for red balloons?'

'Too soon, Apollo,' Kyla said, wiping sweat from her brow. 'You better mind Den doesn't turn up.'

'Ha!' Katrina said. 'If he turns up, it's thirty against one.'

'He wouldn't. *But* everyone will be coming soon,' Apollo said to the girls. 'So when you've finished with that balloon thing, can you put the rest of this stuff on the table?'

'Please remember who you're talking to,' Kyla looked at Apollo quickly. '*You* can make one of your boys do it.'

Apollo laughed and went back upstairs to get ready. 'Garden is looking good,' he said to Sapphire as he walked back into the flat, 'but not as good as you.'

'And not as good as you, when you put your nice clothes on,' Sapphire smiled. 'Quickly though, it's almost seven.'

Apollo kissed Sapphire on the forehead before going to the tiny bathroom and turning the shower on. He stripped off and stepped in, sighing as he felt the cool water run over him. It was a very hot day. He didn't know how Sapphire could bear it.

When he was done, he wrapped a towel around his waist and padded out into the main room. He looked around at the little additions he'd brought to the flat since moving in. There was a poster, the first gift he'd got Sapphire. Then there was the plant, to give the place a bit of life. Obviously he'd brought his TV from his, and his shelf and books.

'What are you thinking?' Sapphire asked from the kitchen sink where she was cooling her wrists under the cold tap, having watched Apollo looking around their flat in a daze.

'It's been one year, hasn't it? To the day,' Apollo asked. 'Since we met.'

'Yeah,' Sapphire said, turning off the tap, walking slowly over to the bed and sitting down. 'It's been the best year of my life. I mean that. Despite all the mess. And Den.'

'Don't worry about Den,' Apollo said, sitting down next to Sapphire.

'I'm not worried about Den,' Sapphire assured him. 'He's not going to do shit. He doesn't even have any friends. Him and which army are going to harm us?'

Apollo turned to look at Sapphire. She looked almost exactly like she did a year ago, when he first fell onto her on the tube. Her face was a little fuller, her eyes shone brighter, and she had a glow to her.

'It's been the best year of my life as well,' Apollo said. 'I've never met a girl like you before, Sapphire.'

It had been quite the year. After turning herself in, and despite all of the high drama, Sapphire had only stayed in a cell for one night. The minute she'd been taken away, Apollo had run to find every Red Rose and Gold Teeth member he could, to ask them to make a statement explaining what happened. And he had spent hours tracking down the footage of the fight that had made its way onto Twitter and Snapchat to use it as evidence.

Even though walking into a police station and cooperating was the last thing any of them wanted to do, the Red Roses did it for Sapphire, and most of the Gold Teeth did it for Apollo. Even Zora, when she'd woken up properly, agreed to say what happened. Even though it meant she got arrested a week after she'd left hospital for having carried a weapon.

Sapphire and Zora both got community service, which they were both still doing, though not together. That was probably for the best.

Sapphire and Apollo spent every single day together. At first he said he was staying over all the time to protect Sapphire from Den. Then, when Sapphire said 'You basically live here' to him, Apollo had gone home, got a few of his things and had made it official.

Speaking of Den, for a while he tried to keep the Gold Teeth together. First he told his boys they wouldn't be safe on the roads without him. And when they laughed that off, he tried to threaten them. They laughed that off too. He started a one-man campaign to scare Sapphire and Apollo. He passed on messages that he was out for them and that they should watch their backs. But nothing ever came of it. Without his crew to back him, Den was nothing.

Sapphire had to stop working at Dawn's café to do her community service, so Apollo had started working there as well as at the record shop. He was tired, but it was worth it. And they needed the money, because two months after he moved in, he and Sapphire found out they were going to be parents.

The day they found out, Sapphire went round to her mum's house to tell her. Sapphire had been terrified. She hadn't spoken to her mum since the incident. Sapphire expected anger, or for her mum to close the door in her face. But instead her mum pulled her in and told her that she'd missed her with every part of her. Then they both cried for ages. Sapphire blamed it on hormones, but her mum knew it was because she finally understood that she'd been forgiven.

It had really been a busy year.

The doorbell rang, pulling the couple out of their moment. It wasn't like these moments didn't happen often, though. They happened every morning and every evening. Apollo Balvin and

Sapphire Light were two of the most head-over-heels-for-each-other people in south London.

'I'll get it,' Sapphire said, rising very slowly. 'You get dressed.'

And so, here we are again. One whole year later. It was a Saturday, around 7 p.m. It was the twenty-sixth of August, and the eve of Notting Hill Carnival. The day had been sunny, and it wasn't getting dark any time soon. London was bristling with summer. The people, the trees, the sounds: they were all alive in a way that only summer can create. Summer gives life to things the other seasons can't fully nourish.

It had been a good time in the Balvin-Light garden. As well as their families, almost all of those formerly known as the Red Roses and those formerly known as the Gold Teeth were present. They had played various games and eaten delicious cake. All but Den, of course.

'Are we doing speeches?' Kyla shouted across the garden. 'If we're doing speeches, I'll do one!'

'You don't need to do any speeches,' Sapphire said, cutting her sister off. She knew Kyla would only start crying and rambling. 'I don't think anyone does speeches at baby showers.'

'I'd like to say something,' Zora said, standing up. As she did, her crop top rode up and showed the large scar on her side.

Everyone was a little bit nervous. Especially Sapphire. The two were on civil terms, but Sapphire suspected that that was only because she was carrying Apollo's child.

'Don't worry, Sapphire. You can breathe out,' Zora said. 'I see you looking all tense and that. I'll keep it short, and keep it nice. I know this day is all about the baby. But because you're the one having the baby, it's about you too.'

Sapphire let out a laugh and Apollo stroked her stomach.

'I just want to thank you, you know. Yeah, I ended up in hospital, but the path I was on wasn't a good one. I could have ended up somewhere worse. And everything that happened, because of you, showed me that. So blessings to you. And to my twin. And to baby Balvin-Light. A powerful union.' With that, Zora raised her glass, and everyone else in the garden raised theirs.

Apart from a few minutes where Sapphire snuck back upstairs and had a nap, everyone danced the night away. Not quite like Carnival, but it was their own celebration of love, life and culture.

About Quick Reads

"Reading is such an important building block for success"
- Jojo Moyes

Quick Reads are short books written by best-selling authors. They are perfect for regular readers and adults reading for pleasure for the first time. Since 2006, over 4.8 million copies of more than 100 titles have been read!

Available to buy in paperback or ebook and to borrow from your local library.

Turn over to find your next Quick Read...

A special thank you to Jojo Moyes
for her generous donation and support of Quick Reads and to **Here Design**.

Quick Reads is part of The Reading Agency, a national charity tackling life's big challenges through the proven power of reading.

www.readingagency.org.uk
@readingagency   #QuickReads

The Reading Agency Ltd. Registered number: 3904882 (England & Wales)
Registered charity number: 1085443 (England & Wales)
Registered Office: Free Word Centre, 60 Farringdon Road, London, EC1R 3GA
The Reading Agency is supported using public funding by Arts Council England.

Find your next Quick Read:
the 2020 series

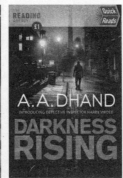

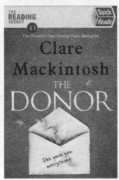

More from Quick Reads

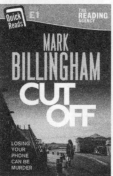

For a complete list of titles and more information
on the authors and stories visit

www.readingagency.org.uk/quickreads

Continue your reading journey

The Reading Agency is here to help keep you
and your family reading:

Challenge yourself to complete six reads
by taking part in **Reading Ahead**
at your local library, college or workplace
readingahead.org.uk

Join **Reading Groups for Everyone** to find a
reading group and discover new books
readinggroups.org.uk

Celebrate reading on **World Book Night**
every year on 23 April
worldbooknight.org

Read with your family as part of the
Summer Reading Challenge
at your local library
summerreadingchallenge.org.uk

For more information, please visit our website:
readingagency.org.uk